MOLLY
&
MILLIE MOOSE
IN THE LAST FRONTIER

HOLLY LILLEY

Balboa Press books may be ordered through booksellers or by contacting:

Balboa Press
A Division of Hay House
1663 Liberty Drive
Bloomington, IN 47403
www.balboapress.com
844-682-1282

Because of the dynamic nature of the Internet, any web addresses or links contained in this book may have changed since publication and may no longer be valid. The views expressed in this work are solely those of the author and do not necessarily reflect the views of the publisher, and the publisher hereby disclaims any responsibility for them.

ISBN: 978-1-9822-5396-7 (sc)
ISBN: 978-1-9822-5395-0 (e)

Library of Congress Control Number: 2020916397

Print information available on the last page.

Balboa Press rev. date: 09/14/2020

BALBOA.PRESS

This book is dedicated to my loves:

Troy Sylus, my Moonpie, I love you to the moon and back, infinity times infinity.

Aby, my Sunshine, I love you forever and always, infinity times infinity.

Kristina Michelle, my Distant Star, I love you always and forever, infinity times infinity.

In a land far, far away, in a place called Alaska where the animals roam and play

Where the snow falls in the winter and the Northern Lights fills the skies.

Where the ice covers the mountains, and the days seems like nights.

While in the summer the fireweed grows, and the sun never sets.

High above at night it glows, as the sun and moon
has met.

There is a moose family that lives in the mountains,

up above the city that lies down below.

Where the water falls like fountains, as the wind gently blows.

The female moose, called a cow, nibbles on some leaves.

While her baby, called a calf, hides behind the trees.

Mama Moose named Molly, stands tall and proud.
While Millie Moose, her baby, hides from the crowds.

Molly and Millie spends their days eating, they are herbivores and only eat plants.

They walk around searching for trees, and if you watch closely you may catch a glance.

Moose usually travel alone, unless they have a baby.

Mama and baby are loving and close.

They share sweet kisses together, as they bump nose to nose.

The baby moose, named Millie, loves to run, jump, and play.

While mama moose, named Molly, watches to keep her safe.

Their front legs are longer than their back legs.

This helps them jump over things.

They just hop up and over it like it was nothing.

They share these mountains with others.

Like bunnies,

birds

and bears.

Molly must be careful and watch over Millie.

Moose must be bear aware.

As the day draws to a close

Molly and Millie are tired and lie down.

Millie curls up next to Molly

And falls asleep without a sound.

Good night Molly and Millie Moose.

Before leaving The Last Frontier, Molly and Millie would like to share some advice with you.

Always remember that when you go searching under the rainbows for treasures,

the rainbows for treasures,

the greatest treasure that you can ever find will be those who love you.

Alaska, The Last Frontier

Lilley's Moments Frozen in Time

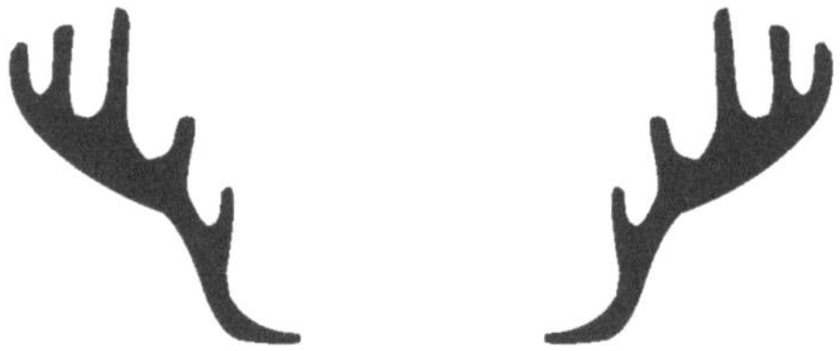

Printed in the United States
By Bookmasters